6 7 8 9 10

15 16 17

1 22 23

28 29 30 3

4 35 36 37

Copyright © 2002 by NordSüd Verlag AG, Zürich, Switzerland.
First published in Switzerland under the title *Der Regenbogenfisch lernt zählen*.
English translation copyright © 2002 by North-South Books Inc., New York

First published in the United States, Great Britain, Canada, Australia and New Zealand in
2002 by North-South Books Inc., an imprint of NordSüd Verlag AG, Zürich, Switzerland.

Distributed in the United States by North-South Books Inc., New York.

Library of Congress Cataloging-in-Publication Data is available.

ISBN-13: 978-0-7358-1716-6 / ISBN-10: 0-7358-1716-2 (trade edition)
10 9 8 7 6 5 4

Printed in China

www.northsouth.com

MARCUS PFISTER

Rainbow Fish
1, 2, 3

NorthSouth BOOKS

NEW YORK / LONDON

How many  yellow scales
does Rainbow Fish have?

Can you count one orange starfish, too?

How many  orange scales does Rainbow Fish have?

Can you count two purple clamshells, too?

How many 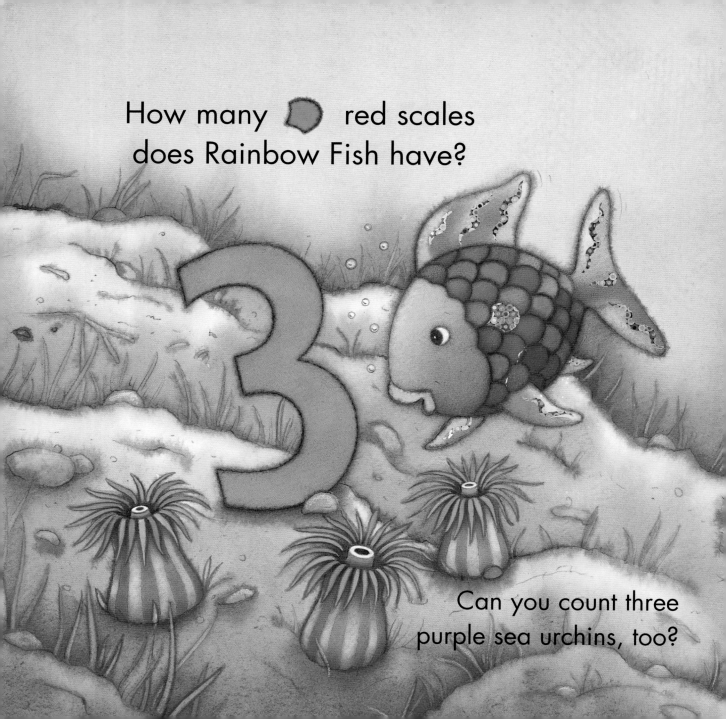 red scales
does Rainbow Fish have?

Can you count three
purple sea urchins, too?

How many  green scales does Rainbow Fish have?

Can you count four orange-and-yellow sea horses, too?

How many  pink scales does Rainbow Fish have?

Can you count five blue conch shells, too?

How many  purple scales
does Rainbow Fish have?

Can you count
six green leaves, too?

How many 🔵 blue scales does Rainbow Fish have?

Can you count seven blue fish, too?

8

How many  purple scales does Rainbow Fish have?

Can you count eight green prickly plants, too?

How many  blue scales
does Rainbow Fish have?
Can you count nine orange crabs, too?

How many  silver scales does Rainbow Fish have?

Can you count ten pretty bubbles, too?